Sacred Dimensions
A Story of Design, Desire & Becoming

by

Amara Larimar

Editor, Christina Marcus

Printed in the United States of America
First Printing, 2026

ISBN 978-1-942385-24-0

To my Framily, you know who you are. They say the people who surround you are a reflection of your spirit. If that's true, then I am abundantly blessed, because each of you reflects light, strength, and love in ways that continually call me higher.

Thank you, Malik, for showing me in real time that growth and tenderness can share the same space in harmony. You are a mirror that I didn't know I needed. You are a steady presence in a storm. You are my quiet muse. A reminder of who I am becoming.

I give thanks for the woman I am and for the woman who is learning to meet her own gaze with courage, audacity, and grace.

Sacred Dimensions
A Story of Design, Desire & Becoming

CHAPTER 1

DISTANT STRUCTURES

The text came just after midnight.

Malik Bilal.

Amara paused and stared at the name as another text popped up. That name alone had a weight to it.

"You still up"

No emoji. No punctuation. Just Malik. Direct, per usual.

She smiled and looked out the window of her loft, the Old Fourth Ward corner of the Beltline. The Beltline glowed like a circuit board. Beneath her, work covered Amara's desk in the form of sketches, budgets, construction submittals, and study materials. Yet the text pulled her attention away from all of it. It had been a while. Not years exactly, but long enough for the space between them to feel... intentional.

Her phone buzzed again.

"I didn't mean to wake you. You crossed my mind."

A part of her smiled. The other part stayed guarded. Malik always knew how to say just enough to pull her in.

They met the next evening at Apogee Tavern, a quiet spot in Inman Park that had not changed in the last decade. Low lights, mismatched furniture, vintage art on the walls, and music humming from hidden speakers. The music was a mix of old soul, underground hip hop, and the kind of Southern rhythm Atlanta never quite let go of. Resonant.

Amara pushed the door open and spotted Malik behind the bar.

He hadn't seen her yet.

He was finishing a drink. Steady hands folding a citrus peel into a curve with the precision of a ritual. His frame was slightly broader now. His beard was more deliberate and sexy. He wore a plain black button-down and dark jeans, nothing flashy, yet the look distinguished him. Malik definitely had his own style. There was a languid sensuality in his movement that hadn't changed.

When he looked up and caught her eye, his face relaxed into something like a smirk.

"Taji."

She raised a brow, smirked back at him, but didn't call him out immediately for calling her Taji. She paused and said, "I see you still lean on old habits, Malik Bilal."

He gestured toward the bar. "Sit. First drink is on me."

"I'm not staying long," she asserted.

"You never do." He chuckled.

Still, she took a seat.

The conversation was easy.

The ease made Amara feel comfortable and uncomfortable at the same time.

They talked about the city, how much it had grown, how some pockets still felt like home. He asked about her latest projects. She gave him the high-level version, careful not to overshare. He listened with interest, nodding occasionally, asking thoughtful questions that reminded her of who she remembered him to be from their architecture school days at Solara.

"You always knew how to stretch a sentence into a story," she teased.

Malik grinned. "Only when I had the right audience."

There was a pause, not awkward, but very full.

He didn't mention architecture. Not yet.

But when he talked about curating drinks, getting to know his clientele, creating new flavor pairings, organizing bar takeovers like design projects, she heard it. The rhythm.

"You ever think about doing something different?" she asked neutrally, keeping her voice light.

He shrugged. He breathed out softly, a sound almost like a laugh, like he was visualizing a new space. "Sometimes," he said. "But I chose this work. I'm good at it. His eyes dipped for a moment, not in doubt, but to someplace deeper than the room where they stood. People feel safe with me. It's a respected craft."

There was more behind his words. Something he didn't offer. Something he guarded, the way a man guards the pieces of himself that make him whole.

"But does it feed your spirit, love?"

Malik glanced at her then. The look was brief, but telling.

"You sound like someone who remembers too much," he said.

She gave a small smile. "Seeing you brings back memories of our college days. I never told you this, but I recognized there was something pulling you away right before you left school. I began to distance myself from you. I knew the pull was greater than me, greater than the studio. More importantly my love and respect for you ran deep. I genuinely wanted you to find what you were looking for and continue your journey of greatness with confidence. I would have complicated things and frustrated myself by staying around you. I remember being sad, but making a choice. I wanted to be a source of joy and peace for you, I never wanted to get in the way of what you needed and deserved. Plus I was soul searching myself."

Malik looked at her deeply like he wanted to respond. He nodded and replied, "Heard."

When it was time to leave, he walked her to the door. Highland Avenue was quiet. It was the kind of fall night that made the air feel like whispers of a distant memory.

"I didn't mean to interrupt anything last night," he said. "I just… wanted to talk to someone who knows the real me."

"I know. I came because I needed the same," she replied.

Amara knew something more was on his mind, but didn't push him for it. Timing is everything. Malik will communicate when he is ready. "It was good to see you, Malik. Love you, friend."

"Love you too, Amara."

He didn't call her Taji again this time. Not out loud at least.

But she felt him call her Taji in the way he looked at her. As if he was searching for *something*… something that had not moved even as everything else had.

CHAPTER 2

RENDERINGS OF THE PAST

Amara paused at her drafting table, the soft scrape of charcoal pulling her back in time. For a moment, her loft around her dissolved, and she was back in the studio where it all began, at the Solara Institute of Architecture in 1999.

The studio smelled like chipboard, glue accelerator, and burnt coffee.

Amara sat at her drafting table. She was doing the nervous leg bounce she did when she was unsettled about something. Her drafter's lamp casted a soft arc over the tracing paper on her table. Outside the windows, the sky was dark and heavy, the campus nearly silent with exception of the sound of crickets. Inside, only a few scattered students remained, heads down, headphones on in quiet focus.

Somewhere near the stairwell, a speaker played low music, jazz with a touch of something futuristic yet old, maybe Herbie Hancock. It filled the space without overpowering it, like a quality film score.

Amara was in her second year. By now, she had learned how to tune out everything, but the lines. Her pencil moved in slow deliberate strokes as she worked through her elevation study for a housing project. Amara preferred working late at night. The silence gave her space to think, to breathe, and to ground herself.

That was when she heard the door open.

She did not need to look up. She already knew who it was by the rhythm of the movement.

Malik.

He moved the same way every time. Quiet, but not cautious. There was a force to his presence, even when he was just crossing a room. He wore his usual NYC hoodie pulled low over his forehead, carried a worn sketchpad under one arm, and held a mechanical drafting pencil behind his ear.

Malik was not enrolled in her section, but somehow, he always ended up in her studio after hours. Always found the desk near hers. Always asked the kind of deep questions professors skipped past in class. And Amara had never asked him to leave.

She waited until he had settled at the desk across from her before speaking.

"Back again?"

He smirked without looking up. "You know this place has the best acoustics at night."

She let the silence sit between them for a moment, then nodded toward his pad. "What are you working on?"

He flipped his sketchbook open and turned it so she could see. A dense, gestural sketch of an open-air library with winding staircases, plants, and light wells.

Her brow lifted. "It's logical, chaotic, and rhythmic at the same time."

"Thanks." Malik said.

"And brave." Amara remarked.

Malik glanced up, genuinely curious. "Brave?"

She nodded. "It's an intelligent design. You're not afraid of risk. Most people are."

He shrugged. "Risk or taking chances is how I find the thing underneath. The core elements."

She leaned over, tapping a portion of the drawing. "This curve right here. It's fighting the structure."

"Maybe the structure needs a fight." Malik chuckled.

Amara gave a small smile and leaned back into her chair.

They worked in tandem after that, speaking in pauses and glances. Occasionally a remark. Sometimes a laugh. When she stood to stretch, he pulled out a second chair, propped up his feet, and placed his sketchpad in his lap like a journal.

Their conversation turned.

They talked about light, about what makes a space feel sacred. About ancestral memory in architecture. About public places that felt more private than home. Amara told him about her childhood library, with its wide windows and creaky floors; how it shaped the way she thought about space and the intersection of light.

Malik told her he liked to draw when the world was quiet.

"It's the only time I can hear myself think," he said. "The only time the pressure is off."

She understood what he meant without needing him to explain. They were not the same, but they shared that need to escape into creation.

"I love cities at night," she said softly. "When everyone's inside, the buildings seem taller. Like they're breathing creatures."

He nodded. "Like they're coming alive."

At some point, the music shifted. Someone had switched to Erykah Badu's *Next Lifetime*.

Erykah Badu's voice settled into the space like incense. Unhurried, swirling on its own path and certain.

Amara kept working, letting the sound settle into her chest. Malik leaned back, listening without comment. The music was a call on their connection. Their response was profound with respect for timing.

Amara's pencil slowed as she listened and breathed. The moment felt like a vignette of time, an arm suspended between her thoughts and breath.

Malik had gone quiet. He was shading something in his sketchbook, long deliberate marks.

Then he looked up. "Can I ask you something?"

She set her pencil down. "Sure."

"Do you think I fit here? I mean... in this program?" His voice was casual, but the question sat with her like bricks on her chest.

She took a moment before answering. "I think you think differently than they want you to think."

"That's a nice way of saying I don't belong."

She met his eyes. "I didn't say that."

Malik gave a slow nod, his expression unreadable. "Sometimes I feel like I'm just pretending to be what they want. And that's not something I'm built for."

Amara watched him carefully. "In a sense we all do that... But you don't have to pretend. You build what you want to see. You shape atmosphere, feeling, and truth. That is a gift most people never experience. That's what makes you truly unique."

She stepped closer, not physically, but in presence.

"Vision is one of your many superpowers. You are divine, Malik. You are built for more than this place allows. I hope you know that."

He looked at her for a long time, then said, quietly, "You're brilliant, you know that?"

She shook her head, brushing it off, "I'm just working."

"No," he said. "You're doing more than that. You see things. You make sense of them. You've got range."

She looked down, then back at him. "So do you. You just haven't decided if you believe it yet."

A few minutes passed in silence. Then he slid his sketchbook across the table to her.

She opened it and something unexpected caught her eye. An abstract drawing, but layered and strong. The lines were sharp and architectural with a feminine curve that felt familiar. A silhouette. Hers.

She laughed gently. "Is this supposed to be me?"

He shrugged, not denying it.

"You know what you are, right?" he asked.

She raised an eyebrow. "Sleep deprived?"

He smiled. "A crown. That's what you are."

She gave him a skeptical look.

He leaned back, tapping the edge of his sketchpad. "Taji."

She blinked. "What?"

"That's what I'm calling you from now on. Taji. It means crown."

Her instinct was to brush it off. But something about the way he said it made her pause. It was not a flirt. It was a naming.

She gave him a half-smile and turned back to her desk.

They kept working, the two of them quietly sketching in their own corners of the same room. The studio faded around them. The air softened.

And Amara, pencil in hand, stole one more glance at him.

They had not kissed. Had never touched beyond a hug. Although the unspoken yearning was obvious, Amara valued him, and chose not to act on her impulsive and growing desires. She remained curious about Malik.

But they had built something.

Something only they could name.

Back then, neither of them knew those nights would live on long after they ended.

CHAPTER 3

DRAWING ON UBUNTU

Amara's phone buzzed.

Unknown number.

She almost ignored it since it was after work hours, but answered anyway. "Still working late, aren't you?"

That tone. Low. Familiar. Disarming.

"Malik?" she said softly, a half-laugh escaping her lips before she even thought about it.

He chuckled. "Thought you'd changed your number by now. Guess some things don't change."

It had been over a year since their night at Apogee Tavern. They hadn't really spoken in depth since then. There had been a quick hello at a mutual friend's cookout at Stone Mountain Park, a few likes on social media, a congratulatory text when she opened her architecture studio. But nothing truly conversational. Nothing direct.

So when his voice reached her now, its quiet timing slipped through the line and settled somewhere deep in her gut.

He was bartending again, he said. A rooftop lounge in the West End. Temporary gig while he explored a few projects. "You should come by," he added. Not as an invitation, but as if it were a natural continuation of their old rhythm. One more studio night that had simply stretched into adulthood.

Amara hesitated for exactly six seconds before saying, "yes".

The Obsidian Rooftop Lounge sat above the West End, quiet and unapologetically deliberate, for those who understood what that part of the city meant. Upon her arrival, Amara noticed overgrown vines tangled through now dimmed string lights, the scent of lemongrass and cigar smoke drifting on the breeze. He spotted her before she saw him; crop top, fitted ankara skirt, and strappy wedges, eyes scanning the crowd like she was studying a floor plan.

When she finally looked his way, time folded in on them.

Time didn't rush backward, it simply expanded, making space for both who they were and who they'd become.

"Amara Sanaa," he said with that crooked grin that used to drive professors crazy because it meant he'd already solved the design problem they were still explaining to the class. "You look and smell like success, love."

She smiled, leaning against the bar. "And you look like a man who got tired of client meetings."

He poured her something golden, bourbon, honey, and something with a floral aroma in a crystal glencairn glass.

"It's called the Sketch Line," he said, setting it down. "Unpredictable. Changes every time I make it."

"Sounds like you," she chuckled.

They talked for hours about old studio nights, the brutal competition in grad school, and what they had lost and learned along the way. Each word carried subtext, each silence a shared rendering of memory.

Then, between sips, he mentioned it.

A concept.

A farm to lifestyle community, a sustainable mixed use wellness development, inspired by African botanicals, and the ritual of healing through design.

"People keep saying sustainability is a trend," Malik said, eyes narrowing in thought. "It's not a trend if it is tradition. My grandmother Alice used to grind shea nuts and moringa leaves behind her apothecary shop. That was her architecture. I want to build and bring back this type of design and practice. Our culture fundamentally has always been the cure."

She smiled and her pulse quickened. She had been studying ethnobotany for years. The work of Dr. George Washington Carver, Dr. Kweku Andoh, Dr. Tanisha Williams, Beronda Montgomery, and the long kept plant rituals of her ancestors was intriguing to her. She was particularly keen on ethnobotany as it relates to traditions in indigenous architecture. She viewed it as the real anthropology. Malik had her full attention and was speaking her language.

"Lately, I've been researching adaptive reuse for wellness developments, with ethnobotany at the foundation, giving us the opportunity to heal both the land and the people," she said, reaching for his napkin. "It opens the door to real generational wealth. Old brick churches, reimagined as sanctuaries of 360° health. You could layer earth and texture like…"

"… like skin," he finished.

They looked at each other.

Something old reignited, not the naïve spark of youth, but the smoldering recognition of mature purpose aligning with desire.

By the end of the night, the napkin between them was filled with sketches; curves of walls, notes about rainwater collection, sensory experiences, and organic finishes. Her handwriting brushed his. His lines intersected hers.

A 3D model was taking shape between Amara and Malik; although to them it looked only like a rough sketch. It was the beginning of something transcendent.

Weeks turned into months.

The napkin became a proposal, the proposal became a partnership. They met in cafés, studios, and over late-night Zoom calls that stretched past midnight. In those hours, they sharpened each other. His questions pushed her further, her insight expanded his vision. Together, they refined ideas, reshaped possibilities, and lifted each other into a kind of brilliance neither could reach alone. Their creative arguments were foreplay disguised as design, heat disguised as process.

They spoke in materials and metaphors:

She talked about light as emotion.

He talked about texture as memory.

Together, they designed spaces that breathed the many languages and cultures of their ancestors. It was as if they were reclaiming what generations were forced to forget.

Amara and Malik created walls that invited the earth to heal you back.

The Ubuntu Village Project was born that way… out of two people seeking restoration through creation. It was the perfect blend of Malik's modern style and Amara's traditional West African aesthetic. It was a refuge that celebrated melanin, soil, and soul. But before it could become anything more than sketches and conviction, it was tested.

The funding call came on a Tuesday afternoon, polished and congratulatory at first. The firm was prepared to commit the capital needed to move Ubuntu Village from vision to construction. But there was a condition. The emphasis on African botanicals, ancestral healing, and cultural reclamation was deemed *too narrow for broader markets*. They suggested reframing it as a *globally inspired wellness development* and softening the *Ubuntu* name to something more neutral. Malik listened without interrupting, his expression unreadable. When the call ended, the room was quiet. He looked at Amara and said evenly, "They want the aesthetic without the ancestry." She did not hesitate. "Then they don't get to fund it." There was no dramatic debate, no scrambling for compromise. Just a long look between two people who understood that their assignment was to honor and restore legacy. That night, instead of revising language to please outsiders, they drafted a new plan;

community backed investment rounds, local partnerships, cooperative ownership models. Smaller checks. A slower build. Deeper roots. It would take longer. It would cost them comfort at times. But Ubuntu would remain intact. And in choosing principle over convenience, something steadier deepened between them, not just ambition, but trust. They weren't just building a development anymore. They were building it the way their ancestors would have, collectively.

The early months were slower than expected. Community meetings replaced investor dinners. Folding chairs, handwritten pledges, elders asking hard questions beneath fluorescent church lights. But the foundation was deeper for it. When Ubuntu finally broke ground, it did so without dilution.

The concept would later spark a lineage of similar developments. It was often compared to predecessors such as Serenbe Community, South Village, KASI, and Agritopia, but none carried the same soul. There was something distinct about the asé Malik and Amara poured into Ubuntu. Little did they know the Ubuntu Village Project would be revered for generations.

When the awards came, neither of them was surprised. Standing side by side ceremony after ceremony, flashbulbs ignited like fireflies, both struggled to hide the quiet current that pulsed beneath the applause.

Once while attending the NAACP Image Awards, Malik leaned close to Amara, his voice low against the noise.

"This… this is what we were meant to build."

She turned toward him, smiling.

"Which part?"

He paused, "All of it."

Her chest tightened. Not from confusion, but knowing. He wasn't just talking about architecture.

Later that night, when they toasted under the same skyline that had once been their dream, and was now their canvas, Amara realized how the line between creation and connection had blurred completely.

The architecture had only been a mirror.

What they were really designing, layer by layer, choice by choice, was a way back.

And for the first time in years, Amara didn't resist it.

CHAPTER 4

BLUEPRINTS OF DESIRE

City Hall East shimmered outside her window, glass towers threaded with bands of neon, drones hummed in quiet patterns like fireflies in the distance. Amara hadn't planned for Malik to end up here, not at her loft, not in her sacred space. Something had shifted after the 2026 National Organization of Minority Architects awards dinner. During the ceremony's last toast, after the easy laughter that bled into private conversation, the pull between them was impossible to ignore.

Now he stood at the edge of her living room, blazer tossed carelessly across a chair, shirt undone at the collar. His presence filled the room the way it always had, but now the energy was wiser, more commanding, certain, and refined. Amara leaned against the glass, her reflection right by his in the night skyline. She thought to herself, "All this divine chocolate smelling so delicious standing this close to me! If he takes one step closer..." Malik turned his body towards Amara as if he heard her unspoken thoughts and took a step towards her. Amara's heart fluttered as the words "Is this happening?" escaped her mouth before she could stop herself. Her voice betrayed her inner thoughts. It wasn't denial or refusal. It was memory, waking up.

Their desire cresting like waves. Anticipation holding its breath.

The air tightened, charged with the kind of magic that arrives without warning, the kind that doesn't ask permission before it begins.

Malik closed the space between them with a gentle tug on the lip of her skirt. His hand found her chin, adjusting it just enough so her eyes locked on his. "We've been saying it for decades without saying it," he murmured, his mouth close enough for her to taste the promise on his breath.

Malik did not go where she expected. His fingers traced the inside of her wrist first, slow enough that she felt her pulse answer him. The touch traveled up her arm, lingering at the soft bend of her elbow, then higher until his palm settled at the back of her neck, just beneath her hairline. Amara gasped softly. That place unraveled her, always had. Malik turned Amara around and kissed her on the back of the neck. She shivered and inhaled deeply.

"So this is how you are starting out Bilal?" she slowly teased.

Warmth gathered low and unmistakable, spreading through her like a remembered song.

"Your body says you are enjoying it," he whispered while gently touching her ear with his lips. Malik's other hand rested at her lower back, not pressing, just holding her there, anchoring her to the moment. The restraint made it worse in the best way. Her body leaned into his before her mind could catch up. She was suddenly acutely aware of her breath, her skin, the arousal building where he had not yet touched. Malik felt it too. The way her body softened, opened, answered. He smiled against her neck, knowing exactly what he was doing, and she realized with the tingle in her spine that she was already undone.

When his lips met hers, it wasn't the clumsy urgency of college nights in the studio. It was slower, deeper, as if they were writing a new language together. His kisses demanded and gave in the same breath, a rhythm of push and pull that undid her further. Amara loved the taste and feel of his lips... soft, full, electric. His mouth, his voice, his kiss lit something in her that had been absent for years.

Her fingers slipped beneath his shirt, tracing the lines of his frame, the years written on his body like a fine aged Mendoza Malbec. They stumbled toward the bedroom, laughter breaking between kisses, no shyness now, no hesitation. Clothes became vignettes on the floor; heels, pants, skirt, shirts, each piece discarded with intention.

On the bed, Malik paused long enough to look at her fully, "You're still Taji," he said softly, reverently. The sound of him saying "Taji" slowly drifted over her skin like heat from a wildfire.

Amara pulled him down to her, lips at his ear. "Let me prove it." She hadn't meant to give in so quickly, but with him, resistance had always been a fragile thing.

What followed was no quick reunion, it was methodical layering. His mouth mapped her body like point clouds, his hands marked curves as if they were blueprints of desire. She answered in kind, exploring him with equal hunger, discovering the places that made him shudder, the angles that bent his control.

There were no boundaries at this point, instead long held fantasies were explored with whispered confessions spilling between breaths. She straddled him, commanding and unafraid, and he let her dominate. In return, he stroked her in a way that carried her to a place she had never been. She lost control and he took control in all the right ways. Deep down she longed for slow, sensual tantric lovemaking, but the moment he took over was pure ecstasy. For the first time, Amara was completely present yet submissive, safe, receptive, and cared for in ways she did not know she needed. There was no need for her to direct the narrative. The moment was raw and honest. She had completely yielded to her desires. Malik knew it from the tone of her moans, from the softness of her surrender. She wanted to be quieter, but that was impossible with Malik. He brought out of her what no one else ever could… The real uninhibited Amara… He brought out Taji.

He flipped her beneath him, showing her what he longed for, and his depth. He set the tempo. Slower. Deeper. As if he were teaching at that moment how to hold them both. The power exchange felt natural, earned, and mutual. She felt herself yield not because she was overpowered, but because she was seen.

By the time dawn softened the skyline, they had rewritten themselves through ardor, murmured confessions, and the lingering language of skin.

Amara lay tangled in sheets and Malik's arm. Her yoni sore and feeling so damn good at the same time. Her mind quiet, settled in a way it hadn't been in years. Malik's hand moved slowly along her back, a calm presence until her breath found its pace again. He kissed her forehead and stayed there a moment longer than necessary, as if making sure she was fully back inside herself. "I am pretty sure we both needed that," he murmured softly.

She paused, let out a deep sigh that sounded more like a moan. Amara felt his thumb trace small circles at her shoulder, grounding, and reassuring. She thanked him quietly and held him closer, fitting herself against his chest. The word friend resonated differently now against the reality of what had just happened, yet Malik didn't pull away or rush the moment. He held her as if nothing needed to be resolved yet. She already longed for more of his touch, but for now, this closeness was enough. It was an added dimension both Amara and Malik finally honored.

Amara's breathing stayed even and slowed like her body was in parasympathetic calm. That alone told her something had changed in her. The old Amara would have been frantic and nervous that she made a mistake. Her past fears had never been about closeness. It had been about losing herself. Questions and fear about what happened, about Malik surfaced, but they did not move her into her old mindset. She had her peace.

Malik was quiet beside her, not distant, just present. He wasn't trying to define the moment or pull her closer than she was ready to go. He let it stand.

The next day her inquisitive nature already wondered how this encounter would shape them and their relationship moving forward. Amara didn't want to lose any of it, she refused to name it. Like her herb garden, she wanted their relationship to hold space for refuge, reflection, and growth.

Days turned into weeks, and the intensity of that night softened into the essence of who they were to each other.

CHAPTER 5

AT THE SUMMIT OF STILLNESS

Amara woke with a heaviness she was unable to pinpoint. It clung to her like Deep South summer humidity; invisible and suffocating. The night had been restless. Her mind chased deadlines, replayed meetings, stressed over credential exams, and invented new worries where they did not belong. By morning, she still felt very unsettled. Tears slid down before she could even form a thought. The kind of crying that wasn't attached to a single reason, but to all the things.

Was it the projects? The weight of what she was building? Or something deeper, like grief she hadn't given space to, or a longing she hadn't dared to name? The uncertainty gnawed at her, and when her hands began trembling from the storm of it, she surrendered. She pushed aside her schedule, her to-do lists, the neat little architecture of her day, and chose only one thing... to escape.

By noon she stood at the base of Stone Mountain, its vast granite face rising like a monument older than memory itself. She climbed slowly, her breath syncing with each step, until the world below shrank into a blur of trees and roads. At the summit, she sat open legged on warm rock, the horizon stretching infinitely around her. The city was just a shimmer in the distance, but up here, silence held court.

She closed her eyes. She let the tears come again, but this time they felt different. Not frantic. Not crushing. Cleansing.

The mountain absorbed it all; her fear, her fatigue, the fragments of dreams and desires she left unsaid. And in the stillness, she felt her body soften, her breath deepen, and her spirit became quiet.

When she descended, she knew where to go next; the small crystal shop on the corner of Main Street and Mountain Gate Street. Its walls hummed low with resetting energy, shelves glinting with quartz, agates, and stones kissed by the earth's oldest winds, fires, and waters. Today she wasn't browsing. Amara was searching. She wanted what would ground her, what would ease her heart, bring back her pleasure, ground her spirit, and remind her of her own capacity to heal.

Her hand moved first to Golden Healer, the warm stone humming with balance and renewal. A silent vow that she could keep standing regardless of the storm. Then to Purpurite, its violet luster carrying clarity and grounding, like roots anchoring her even as her spirit stretched upward. She traced the delicate patterns of Flower Agate, clear, opaque, soft and nurturing, reminding her that joy could bloom again in places that felt barren. And when her fingers closed around Rhodochrosite, her pulse shifted. This one was alive. It radiated warmth, desire, the invitation to feel, AND to allow pleasure, creativity, intimacy alongside love. She held it longer than the others, letting its vibration soften the last brittle edges inside her.

She lingered near the display, thinking of Malik. Something for him... a stone that would carry strength, grounding, and protection. She almost chose one, but stopped. Not yet. Healing herself had to come first. After all Amara desired to keep herself first so that she could show up as her whole self for people a part of her everyday life.

Still, the thought of him stirred something resolute inside her. As if her spirit already knew what her mind refused to admit... that Malik would need her light just as Amara would need his strength.

Walking out of the shop, crystals gathered in a small batik pouch, she felt lighter. The ache wasn't gone, but it no longer ruled her. She tucked the bag close to her chest and whispered to herself: "You are deserving of ease, pleasure, and grounding. These crystals will keep you on your healing journey and bring you authentic joy, peace, and power."

CHAPTER 6

INTERVALS

The city was still.

Morning light broke through the blinds, slicing her room into warm stripes of gold. Amara sat on the edge of her bed, robe loosely tied, chamomile tea untouched on the nightstand. Her mind replayed every fragment of that erotic night with Malik...the way he looked into her eyes, the way his voice dropped when he laughed, the softness that existed between the pauses, the heat that rose like something ancient and unspoken.

It had happened.

And now she couldn't stop feeling it. The way he caressed and stroked her and her undeniable truth underneath it.

A part of her couldn't believe she had let it happen, another part longed for more.

And then there was the quiet fear, the one that whispered what if this ruins everything?

Their friendship meant everything to her, but oddly enough she was willing to risk it. Amara knew they both had the maturity to work through any challenge. The friendship was far from ordinary; it was the kind of bond built over years of pure fun, shared work, creative trust, and unspoken understanding. They moved in rhythm even when words failed. To lose that ease, to risk it for desire felt dangerous, but so damn good at the same time. It felt like strength.

In the stillness of morning, her body remembered him.

And her heart remembered what it felt like to be seen and kept safe. Something Amara lacked in her past relationships, although it should have been a given. It took a friend to show her.

In the days that followed, Malik had been different not drastically, but in ways that were felt more than seen. His hugs lingered. His hands found her waist under the guise of a smile and she liked it. Once, while parting ways Malik kissed Amara on the back of her neck. This unraveled her in ways she did not understand. It felt like a soft and seductive secret meant only for her.

And then, one evening, he said that he desired intimacy.

He didn't say with whom. She questioned with whom. But the why was understood by Amara. It was a struggle to admit, but Amara desired true intimacy for herself and with Malik. After Malik spoke, the words hung in the air, thick with possibility and danger.

Amara only smiled in response, yet a potent feeling rose inside her.

His words helped to unlock the truth in her. Inner intimacy was opportunity. It opened roads to know self without performance, feel without judgement, honor intuition, ancestral memory, and authentic connections.

His words also reminded her of his past; the women, the charm, the way he could pull someone close, and make her believe she was the only one.

Amara was not naïve. She had seen Malik through seasons of brilliance, straight wilding and a mix of both. He was magnetic, a man of vision, creation, and control. But this awakening wasn't about his need to control Amara. This dawning was about radical honesty with Malik and herself.

And the truth was, she didn't want a label. She didn't want to be his object or fit into a box that could break later.

She wanted intimacy. A real, quiet, consistent connection. To be understood. To share thoughts that stretched into dawn. To feel safe in letting go with him without losing herself in the process. Amara wanted to be met with truth and not roles. Oddly enough this dynamic was already present in their friendship, but Amara wanted it to be more consistent and rooted in their love for one another.

She didn't know how to share these feelings with him.

So she said nothing.

Instead, she turned inward to process her thoughts.

Amara worked harder. She painted. She designed. She studied. She wrote. She meditated at sunrise and let her emotions spill across her sketch book.

Each drawn line became a confession: the curve of a wall, the softness of light, the tension between shadow and form.

As she created, Amara began to see something new.

That her desire wasn't just for Malik, it was for wholeness. For the space between freedom and connection. For the balance of being seen, held, and still belonging to herself.

Malik had awakened something, yes, but what he awakened was already hers.

That night, she lit a candle and burned purple sage from her herb garden. She sat cross-legged on the floor, journal open, pen poised like a key waiting to unlock her thoughts. The page stared back, empty, and forgiving. She wrote slowly at first:

Damn, I miss him, not the touch, but the ease. The knowing.

I keep asking myself: what is it that I really want? I think it's presence. I feel it is peace.

Maybe intimacy isn't something he gives me totally lol. But I want to share that with him. Maybe it's something I learn to hold, even when he is not around. I want him, but don't want to be dependent on or possessive of him. I desire interdependence. I just want to be with Malik on our own terms.

She paused, the candle flickering beside her, wax pooling like melted gold.

I love our friendship. I want to honor it. I don't want to lose it. And yet, I don't want to unfeel what I feel.

I fell for the safety, the security, the quiet confidence Malik has always had in me. He pours into me. Others have done that too, but this feels different. Maybe I'm struggling because I can't control it, like everything else. I can't reason it away or will it back into something manageable.

What is it about Malik? And what do you do with a feeling like this?

There is a longing, an urgency, to do something with it. But timing matters. It always does. The restraint is nagging and frustrating, and still, I care enough to say nothing. To let it exist without disrupting what we are building, without standing in the way of his dreams or mine. But is saying nothing the real disruption?

And yet, part of me wants to say eff it all. To say forget it and tell him everything. Because I am joy, and I want to share it.

I didn't plan for this. This growing thing was never my intention. But it's here, and I don't yet know what to do with it. I am fumbling on the inside, wanting to move with intention, to stay measured, to make only calculated choices. Maybe I just for once go with the flow.

Maybe this is a glimpse of freedom.

Loving without owning.

Wanting without demanding.

Feeling without fear.

When she finished, she closed the journal gently, and pressed her palm to the cover, as if sealing a promise.

Then she whispered into the quiet,

"I desire to love and be loved deeply. Safely. Healthy. Powerfully. Peacefully. Joyously."

Outside, Atlanta glowed violet against the night. As Amara watched the city hum with after-hours activity, she realized she was not waiting on Malik.

She was building herself, beam by beam, truth by truth. Intimacy began not with Malik's touch, but with the courage to be completely honest with her own heart.

CHAPTER 7

INTERSTITIAL SPACE

Malik had gone quiet again.

Not absent. Just…elsewhere.

Amara knew the rhythm of his disappearances all too well. College taught her that about him. They never came with warnings, only a soft dimming of his light. His presence slowed, his conversation became few, and measured. Malik was still present in body, but Amara could tell his spirit was wandering, sorting through storms only he could see. This felt like déjà vu to her.

They had been winning professionally. Yet she sensed that something within the success unsettled him. That Malik was reckoning with himself. Amara's dad would often say to her "To whom much is given, much is required." Greatness had a strange cost, and Amara could feel Malik paying for it.

Still, she missed him; his laugh, the weight of his presence, the way his silence steadied her heartbeat when the world felt chaotic. Now that silence only echoed like an unfinished space.

That night, she turned on the playlist she wasn't supposed to have made.

The one she built from the songs that reminded her of him.

The first notes of the bass guitar and drums from Cleo Sol's *When I'm in Your Arms* curled around her like breath. She closed her eyes, listened and imagined the warmth of him standing behind her, their reflections blending in the mirror. She could almost feel his hands at her waist, tracing the places only he knew how to read. His scent, deep, woodsy, clean, wrapping her in memory. She remembered the way he would look at her like she was something sacred, something to be studied, and savored, not rushed.

Her body tensed at the thought, not from hunger alone, but from the turn on of being seen completely. She could feel him in the space between her ribs, as if desire itself carried his name.

The next song transitioned.

Her pulse matched the rhythm.

She imagined Malik leaning against her doorframe with a calm and knowing look in his eyes. He didn't speak. He never had to utter a word. His silence did the work, a slow invitation that said come here without a word. He embodied ease and pleasure.

She imagined the sound of his favorite whisky being poured, the pause before he took a sip and looked at her, that unspoken challenge lingering in the air. His gaze was deliberate, heavy enough to make her forget her composure.

In that dreamspace, his hand found her jaw. He studied her face the way an artist studies light, memorizing every detail before touching the canvas. When his thumb brushed her lower lip, her breath caught.

Nothing and yet everything happened in that moment.

Do You Feel Me Wanting You? pulsed through the speakers low and slow, like heartbeat and breath woven together.

Amara sank deeper into the fantasy, Malik's calm unraveling, her restraint dissolving. They didn't rush. They moved in that sacred space between control and surrender, where every exhale felt like a promise and every whisper carried deep history.

The imagined air was thick with their wanting, not wild, but reverent. He had learned her rhythm, how to meet her without conquering her. She felt that in the way his energy filled the room. How his presence said *Sawubona*, an isiZulu greeting. A deeper way to say *I see you and honor your past, present, and future selves.* She missed that version of him, the one who made silence feel like music, who could undo her simply by looking.

Miles away, Malik sat alone, *Midnight Alchemy* by My Boy Arlo playing softly on his Tidal playlist. The night hummed with the same sultry electricity as he contemplated Amara. To him, her gift was midnight alchemy: the quiet art of transforming chaos and darkness into sacred refuge for herself, for them, and for the community she gathered without force. He poured a glass of Malbec he never intended to drink, watching the red swirl as if it held answers.

He thought of Amara's smile, the way it made his guard drop, the way she met him with both softness and fire. He craved that equilibrium; the peace of love without performance, the depth of desire without the noise. No need for his or her representatives to present themselves.

He wasn't avoiding her. He was avoiding the part of himself that felt too much.

Still, when he closed his eyes, he felt her. He imagined her skin, the cadence of her breathing, her quiet pull that made his composure tremble.

When MeelaRue's *Talk to My Body* began on Amara's playlist, the night shifted…

Amara sat on her bed, lost somewhere between memory and imagination. Malik exhaled, miles away, feeling her presence softly stir across his neck without knowing why.

They were both in that liminal space. Apart yet bound, both pretending not to long for each other. Neither would admit it. But undeniably, both would feel it.

And when they saw each other again days later, at a crowded American Institute of Architects gathering, nothing was said. But every glance lingered too long. Every laugh carried a pulse beneath it.

When their eyes met, time bent. The noise around them faded, replaced by that same quiet slow burning heat that was too impossibly haute to ignore.

They didn't touch. There was no need.

Everyone around them could feel the intensity.

The ionic charge moved between them restrained, alive, and undeniable.

CHAPTER 8

SILENCE

Malik had learned that silence was a language all its own.

He used to fear it, mistook it for absence, but now he knew it was where truth waited.

Lately, that truth had been hard to sit with. He found himself with angst and filling his time with boxing drills, playing dominoes, leather working, and whatever distraction he could think of.

Success had come in waves; new contracts, new attention, and new responsibilities. Each wave increased the pressure to perform. People read his calm as confidence, his stillness as control. But inside, Malik felt like he was rebuilding himself again and again, searching for a version of peace that didn't cost so much.

He needed space, not from Amara, not from the world, but from the noise inside his own head.

He would often wake before dawn, the city still dark and unformed, and sit with his Yirgacheffe coffee in silence. No music. No phone. No sketchbook. Just the hum of the refrigerator and the city. He would think about what it meant to be needed, what it meant to give, and how the edges of who he was often became blurred in the giving.

That was what scared him most, how easily he could lose himself inside someone else's light. A lesson etched into him by past loves, where devotion quietly turned into the demand to shrink himself.

Taji's face came to him often in those quiet mornings. The way she listened, the sharpness of her questions, the warmth behind her teasing. He missed her, deeply, privately. But he also knew he couldn't show up half-whole for her or anyone else for that matter.

He was trying to understand the man he was becoming, one who led with intention, not reaction. One who no longer used success to drown out uncertainty. One who wanted to love without losing balance.

He was becoming a man who moved deliberately. Success no longer anesthetized his doubts. It clarified them. Malik had learned how to hold power without letting it spill into ego, fear, or force.

And that work, he realized, required solitude.

It wasn't punishment, or retreat. It was an internal level setting. It was healing.

Still, he could feel her everywhere.

In his studio, where the echo of her laughter seemed to linger.

In his truck, when a certain song came on and his chest tightened.

In the quiet, when the world slowed enough for longing to speak.

He remembered their last conversation, the half-smiles, the weight of everything unspoken. She'd said she understood his need for space, but he knew it still hurt her. It hurt him too.

Malik didn't want Amara to mistake distance for disinterest. But explaining his silence felt like breaking it, and he wasn't ready for that step yet.

Malik thought of his father then, a man who loved through presence, who believed showing up was a language of its own. That quiet pride of the Baby Boomer generation had filled their home with steadiness and a grounded kind of love. It taught Malik endurance, loyalty, and the strength of staying. From that foundation, Malik learned not only how to stand, but how to soften. He carried his father's strength forward. Malik chose to name his feelings, to offer tenderness openly, and to let vulnerability become another form of courage.

And yet, here he was, quiet, thoughtful, and not asking.

Maybe these feelings were signs of growth. Not easy. Not heroic. Just consistent. The slow reconstruction of self.

He wanted Amara to see that the distance wasn't a wall, it was scaffolding. A temporary frame around something still being built.

He hoped she would be patient enough to see what emerged.

That night, he wrote in his sketchbook:

I'M LEARNING HOW TO HOLD PEACE WITHOUT LOSING PASSION.

HOW TO BE STILL WITHOUT DISAPPEARING.

HOW TO WANT WITHOUT NEEDING RESCUE.

He closed the sketchbook and looked out at the city, its lights scattered like thoughts he was unable to catch.

Somewhere out there, he knew, Amara was probably awake too. Maybe listening to the same late-night silence. Maybe thinking of him.

He smiled, faintly.

Love, he realized, wasn't always about closeness.

Sometimes it was about the courage to build alone,

so that when you finally return,

you come back whole.

CHAPTER 9

NIGHT WORK

Trace paper curls on the drafting table.

J Dilla instrumentals on vinyl play in the corner, all beats and hush.

Amara stands at the threshold and waits for her courage to catch up. Malik looks up from a sketch, stillness easing over his shoulders when he sees her. Neither of them rushes the moment. He rises. She steps inside. The door clicks shut behind her and the room feels smaller in a good way.

"Hi," she says.

"Hi Taji," he answers with a smirk.

Silence follows, not empty, just full. It's the kind of quiet that holds space for them just to be.

"I brought you the latest site photos from Ubuntu Village," she adds, lifting a slim folder. It is an excuse and both of them knew it. Because who takes the time to print digital pictures these days? It was painfully obvious that she made an excuse to see him. But she needed no excuse. Malik was always just as happy to see her as she was to see him.

He takes it and sets it aside without looking. "Thank you for coming."

She walks past him, fingers brushing the edge of his table. She takes notice of the studio. Coffee rings. Graphite dust. A simple pencil aligned with an architect's scale like well placed art. She inhales the scent of cedar shavings, smoky myrrh resin, and something that is only him. He circles to the other side and sits at the table.

"How are you," she asks.

"I am working," he says, then softens. "I am trying."

The vinyl whispers. Sirens blare in the distance. Amara leans into the desk and his eyes follow the angle of her lips then eyes. Malik looks calm, but the air around him has an undertow. She feels it in her chest.

"Your drawings look different," she says. "Quieter. Surer."

"I am learning to be careful with what I ask for," he replies. "And how I build it."

They hold the thought together. He slides a sketch toward her. An elevation, clean, and simple. She anchors it with her fingertips and he watches the way her touch holds the paper.

"I missed this," she says. "Being here."

He does not hide his answer. "Me too."

They don't move close yet. They let the wanting linger without swallowing the room. A monarch butterfly outside catches their attention, taps the window once, then twice, a small percussion. They both smile. Malik says, "A butterfly at night feels like a symbolic message". After it passes by, Amara steps to Malik's pinup wall and studies a set of charcoal sketches. He stands at her shoulder with a carefully calculated space between them. The warmth of him finds her anyway.

"You have been far," she says.

"I needed to listen to the parts of me that remain silent when I am busy," he says. "I did not want to bring you the noise."

She takes a moment to process his answer and asks, "And what did you hear?"

"That I want peace with the same intensity I want you," he says, voice low. "That both are possible if I pace myself."

Her throat tightens. His truth landed loud and sat beside hers… Amara turned to him and the space narrows. Close enough to feel the rhythm of his breathing.

"I tried not to miss you," she says. "I failed. I found myself thinking of you when the day went quiet. I wanted your company. Your touch. I wanted the simple things too. A late conversation. A shoulder. The way you make a room feel like a place of rest and ease."

He closed his eyes slowly, inhaled deeply, and opened them again. "I have wanted all of that with you," he says. "I still do."

They say nothing for several seconds. The record crackles. The city murmurs. The studio holds their heat without tipping into fire.

"I was afraid, friend," she admitted. The words came slowly, but they were owned. "I was afraid that if we crossed the line, we would lose what we already had. It is not that I doubt you or your love. I simply understand the cost of lost love now, having paid for it before. Afraid of wanting more than I knew how to hold, more than we knew how to carry together. No one wants to be in love alone."

She let the truth settle, unflinching. Then she claimed the other half of it. By now she understood that fear had never been her weakness. It was discernment, sharpened by time. The kind that only comes after you have survived your own silence. Amara had learned when to pause, but also when to step forward without apology. Wanting was not recklessness. Wanting was a messenger. And this time, she chose to honor it.

Malik responds thoughtfully with a deep inhale and an exhale before speaking. "I am afraid of that too," he says. "I am afraid of breaking the good thing we built, because the timing is not perfect. I am afraid of reaching for you without giving you what you deserve."

"Malik, here is my truth. I love you deeply. You move through this world with a truth most people never outwardly speak of. You lead with conviction, but you also listen, and act with a special tenderness. You are like a quiet cleansing storm and a sanctuary to me. Your vulnerability, when you allow me to witness it, is an absolute privilege that I don't take lightly. I love the way your mind sharpens mine, the way your presence calms me, and the way you make freedom feel like something I can run to, not run from. You challenge me, refine me, let me rise. I love the depth in you; the grit, the brilliance, the many battles you overcome quietly and without ego. I love how you look at me like you see every version of who I've been and who I'm becoming. Loving you feels like recognizing and honoring a frequency in myself that I have always carried."

Amara did not know what to expect from Malik in response. But she was relieved to share her truth with him.

Her eyes shine and her shoulders lower, as if the truth itself loosened a tight knot. He lifts his hand, stops halfway, and waits. She inhales deeply and tilts her head upward to release. He touches her cheek with the gentleness of a promise and anticipation. His thumb rests at the edge of her cheek. Her hand rises to his hands and stays there, light but not pushing away.

"This is how I want it," he says. "Present. Clear. Authentic. No noise."

She nods. "Me too. I don't like noise. Noise is too chaotic for me. And chaos is the love child of haste. Clarity, peace, and steadiness is my preferred residency. "

They stand in that agreement, bodies remembering how to be near without rushing to prove anything. His palm slides to the side of her neck and her breath grows deeper and warmer. She steps the last inch closer, not for a kiss, not for anything that would break the careful balance, but for the gravity of two people finally sharing their truths face to face.

"I want to share something deeper with you," she says.

Malik answers with a nod and smile. "You often say you feel safe with me. My reply is that is how it should be. We should keep each other safe. I am not going anywhere and would be honored to continue to grow with you," he says. The words feel courageous, cliché yet pure all at the same time. "We move with authenticity."

Her forehead finds his chest. His chin rests in her hair. They hold each other and listen to the record till the end of the song. When the last beat fades, they step apart, eyes still tethered to each other.

"What do we do now?" she asks.

He gestures to the table and they move towards it. "We don't force it. We embrace the moment. We keep open communication. We keep building."

She smiles. "Mmmm, we keep building."

He picks up a pencil and slides a clean sheet toward her. She takes it. Side by side, they draw the first lines of something they both want. The studio breathes with them. The city goes on shining. And for the first time in weeks, the quiet between them feels like a sacred intention they can keep.

About the Author

Amara Larimar is an architect, visual artist, and storyteller who believes that stories, like spaces, shape how we feel, heal, and become. Her work lives at the intersection of design, memory, ancestral wisdom, and love.

Through her writing, Amara explores intimacy, identity, and the courage it takes to live truthfully. Her stories are known for their emotional depth, sensual subtlety, and reflection on the unseen architecture of human connection.

When she is not writing, she creates through photography, wellness-centered design, and multidisciplinary projects that honor culture, beauty, and inner transformation.

She writes to remind readers that becoming is a sacred act.

www.ingramcontent.com/pod-product-compliance
Lightning Source LLC
Chambersburg PA
CBHW050835180626
46814CB00004B/1627